LAGRANGE PARK PUBLIC LIBRARY DISTRICT

3 6086 00273 7093

W9-BRD-011

SEP - - 2020

WITHDRAWN

LA GRANGE PARK PUBLIC
LIBRARY DISTRICT
555 N. LA GRANGE ROAD
LA GRANGE PARK, IL 60526

AlMonD

ALMOND

ALLEN SAY

SCHOLASTIC PRESS · NEW YORK

Copyright © 2020 by Allen Say

All rights reserved. Published by Scholastic Press, an imprint of
Scholastic Inc., *Publishers since 1920.* SCHOLASTIC, SCHOLASTIC PRESS,
and associated logos are trademarks and/or registered trademarks of Scholastic Inc.

The publisher does not have any control over and does not assume any responsibility
for author or third-party websites or their content.

No part of this publication may be reproduced, stored in a retrieval system, or transmitted in any
form or by any means, electronic, mechanical, photocopying, recording, or otherwise, without written
permission of the publisher. For information regarding permission, write to
Scholastic Inc., Attention: Permissions Department, 557 Broadway, New York, NY 10012.

This book is a work of fiction. Names, characters, places, and incidents are either the product of the
author's imagination or are used fictitiously, and any resemblance to actual persons, living or dead,
business establishments, events, or locales is entirely coincidental.

Library of Congress Cataloging-in-Publication Data available
ISBN 978-1-338-30037-6

10 9 8 7 6 5 4 3 2 1   20 21 22 23 24
Printed in Malaysia 108
First edition, March 2020

The text type was set in Adobe Garamond Pro.
The display type was set in Monotype Fournier Regular.
The illustrations were created using charcoal, pastel, and photographs.
Book design by Charles Kreloff and David Saylor

For Kalia and Agatha Day Olson

After the New Girl came to school, all the other
students disappeared from Almond's eyes.

The New Girl could play "Flight of the Bumblebee" so
fast that Almond couldn't see the bee.

But she could hear it flying from flower to flower,
drinking nectar, dancing high and low, fast, fast, fast.

"Why did she come to my school?" Almond asked her mother.

"How does she do it?"

"She is talented," said her mother.

"Everyone says the New Girl is a genius," said Almond.

"All they say about me is that I have beautiful hair."

"You will find your talent," said her mother. "Sometimes it takes time."

"Did you find yours?" asked Almond.

"I thought I wanted to be a potter," said her mother. "But then I had you and had to get a job instead of making pots."

"So I am your talent," said Almond.

"The very best," said her mother.

Every day Almond stood under the New Girl's
window and listened to her play. The music was always
the same. The bumblebee flew faster and faster.

One day the teacher announced a class play. "With your beautiful hair you will play Rapunzel," she said to Almond.

Hair is all I have, Almond thought.

"I can't," she whispered. "I have no talent."

"You will be wonderful," said the teacher. "Trust me.
I'll read you the lines. You have a very good memory."

The day of the play arrived. Almond pretended she was a princess named Rapunzel.

She looked out the tower window
and wished she was not alone. She
heard the New Girl's violin. It was
not the bee music.

It was new. It was about a princess who
wanted to travel — to find her talent and be happy.
Almond listened with all her heart.
The audience clapped and clapped.

"You were wonderful!" said her mother. "A natural actress," said the teacher.

"I am not an actress. I don't know how to act. I have no talent."

"Acting is pretending," said the New Girl. "You are a good pretender.
If I weren't going away to a music school we could be friends."

The next day was Saturday. It rained all day.
Almond's violin made no sound.

She stood at her window and watched the crows, circling and twirling and playing like children in the meadow. "You can't sing and you don't have bright feathers," she said.

"But you are happy in the wind and the rain . . .
I wish I could be like you . . ."

And suddenly Almond was flying with the crows —
over the city, over the country, over the sea.
 Swooping and diving and flying. Almond pretended
to be a crow — and she was a crow.

Then she was back at her window — a girl again.

I wonder what else I could be, she thought. *The New Girl said I was a good pretender. She didn't talk about my hair. She thought I was an actress. I thought I was Rapunzel. I thought I was a crow. Maybe I could really learn to act . . .*

Almond ran to tell her mother.

"My darling talent!" said her mother. "An actress!"

And they hugged each other.